Destiny's End

KATHRYN LEO

ISBN: 978-1-959493-59-4 (sc)
ISBN: 978-1-959493-58-7 (ebk)

In a last-minute effort to calm her nerves, Sarah took a deep breath in, counted to ten in her mind, and then exhaled. Before she could open her eyes again to regain awareness of her surroundings she heard the announcement being made to welcome her onto the stage. "It is with my greatest pleasure to welcome you the inventor of the hyper series Professor Sarah Sully. Sarah walked on the stage filled with the sound of thirty people clapping with joy and then ceased with silence.

"I welcome you all here today for the unveiling of my latest hyperdrive series known as MAX." Sarah noticed a glimmer of confusion on one of the spectators' faces. She smiled with delight. "MAX is short for magnified amorphous xenon" "It's also named after my dog Max who celebrates his first birthday today". The audience laughs as the tension of everyone in the room eases.

"As you all know I am the inventor of the hyper series technology. It has been fifty years since the hyper series my father started working on understanding space and time travel. The Hyper series has given us the ability to hyper jump in the distance which means to travel a large distance in a fraction of the time. The last model has given us the ability to travel safely back in time for twenty-four hours which is called the hyper jump in time. As you know the hyper series revolutionised transporting people to the other side of the world within five seconds and traveling back twenty-four hours in time has revolutionised our understanding of time and has proven to be a vital tool for forensic investigation.

"Over the last twenty-five years the hyper series has changed society for the better. I would like to proceed with the unveiling". Sarah turned her back to the audience to watch the raising of the curtains. There it was, MAX, a small insipid silver generator, not much to look at but powerful enough to generate a large star gate to fit twenty people through at once. The Audience broke out in applause, followed by sounds of soft chatting "As you are all probably asking yourselves now, what will it achieve? MAX is a further expansion to my last model" One of the audience interrupted before Sarah had the chance to continue. "I don't understand another time machine. For how long? 48? 70 hours? I mean what would that prove?" "Longer!" she continued breaking the man's interruption. "A hypertime jump with this model will send you eighty years back in time." Expecting another round of applause, all Sarah heard were the sounds of gasping and soft chattering, then silence.

Sarah was caught off guard, failing to know how to continue the rest of her presentation. She felt frustrated with the audience's lack of enthusiasm. "I'm sorry, but is there a problem" directing the question to no one in particular. The member of the press raised his hand. "Yes," said the same man. "Fear is the problem" "Fear?" she said. "Yes, the people fear time travel". Sarah laughed, again breaking the man's conversation "Time travel has been around for a while now and nothing has ever gone wrong." she paused for a while expecting further questions from the audience, but there was only silence; "So what is the fear?"

Two Years Later

As Ben woke up to his alarm, as he had always done. His dream was quickly draining away from his mind; he reached over to turn his alarm off. Ben always allowed himself fifteen minutes laying in bed before getting up. Although it was Ben's day off from work there was no rest for a Professor of History at Winston University he had a full day marking papers and catching up on journals. But before he commenced his busy day, he made a morning routine of sitting on his favorite rocking chair while he drank his cup of hot filter coffee while listening to his voicemail box which was called Victor. "Good morning Ben". "Hello Victor, what do we have for this morning?". "You have two new messages for today. The first message is from your supervisor for your approval of the two weeks' leave you requested.". "Your next message from time Travelex. Your application for time travel deployment has been accepted. You are to contact time Travelex as soon as possible." "Thanks, Victor" It was surreal to Ben that he was chosen to be a candidate for time travel. Travelex was a new corporate form that specialised in researching and performing time travel. The next venture is to choose twenty candidates to hyperjump eighty years back into time. They picked twenty people from various professions and as a history Professor, Ben was one of the candidates chosen.

He decided to celebrate the news with a cup of coffee followed by a long hot bath before commencing the day with marking papers. The assignment was an essay that asked its students to pick and write about why they would change in history and why. Some students responded by wanting to change various moments of the last fifty years which included terror attacks, car accidents, and various crimes. One paper stood out from the rest which read "If I could change one part of history I would change my own. Three years ago I had fallen in love with a girl and we spent two years happy years together without a fight. One day she said she wanted to move in together but I wanted my space and we had a huge fight. I went alone to a party that night and cheated on her. She found out through friends that I cheated and she committed suicide. If I could change anything I would not have cheated on her but now I have to live the rest of my life in pain." Thinking of that story Ben thought of his own. He had lost his fiancé in a car accident seven years ago and has lived in solidarity since.

The next day Ben arrived at the Travelex building where a personal assistant was waiting for him. He was taken around the centre for a tour of the corporation. He was taken to a lecture theatre where he was met with the other nineteen candidates and they were given a presentation about the achievements of Travelex and time travel. After the presentation, they were given a briefing about their mission. Their mission was the purpose of hyper jump eighty years back in time which has never been achieved before now. They spent the rest of the day learning about what to expect from jumping back far into time and the safety procedures required. They were each given a vest fitted with a tracking device and a communication device.

The following day was another day of preparation. As soon as the day started they were all shown in a large conference room for another presentation. Ben was surrounded by all of the chosen candidates he had time to get to mingle before the presentation began. He mingled with professors of physiology, medicine, sociology, and political science.

The presentation began with the coordinator of the mission trying to direct all of the candidates to the seating. "Good morning everyone, please I wish you all to your seating so we can begin the presentation." "Welcome my name is Roger and I am the co-coordinator for the mission." "As you are aware you have been chosen as a pioneer for the long time travel experience. Time travel has been around for many years now and it has led to many great changes around the world. People are slowly getting comfortable with the idea of time travel. Fear has been the delay for time travel endeavors. We have chosen twenty people from various professions to explore our history. We hope to eliminate the fear of time travel and expand its purpose."

"May I please introduce to you Professor Sarah Sully the inventor of the time travelling generator MAX." "Thank you. Today I will talk about what you will experience when you travel back in time. When you travel back in time you will enter a new world. This is a world for our time that has already been written. When a person travels in time they are enclosed in a time bubble. This means for any person, living or dead objects can't interact with the person that is experiencing time travel. The person is therefore like a wandering ghost. People, now there are talking about those who experience ghost haunting could have all along been time travellers."

After the presentation, the group stopped for lunch. Ben wasn't up for mingling with the other peers, for nerves started to kick in. He noticed a coffee machine in the corner of the room and started to make his way toward it. After finishing his last drop of black coffee he heard a voice coming from behind him. "Hello Sir" Ben turned around, it was Professor Sully. "Hello Professor, please call me Ben." "Hello Ben, you must be the history professor, I'm so glad I have finally met you. "Really, I er" "Nervous" "Yes sorry my thoughts are scattered at the moment, I've been teaching history for twenty years now, and here I have been chosen as a pioneer to travel back into time". "It's OK. You will be Safe. Remember you can communicate with me while you have jumped back. It is the big day tomorrow and you will be equipped with all you need that will last you ninety-six hours of exploration." "The date will be the twelfth of June 2030 and as you know already there have been big changes that occurred during the last eighty years so the world will seem quite different."

Ben fell in for a minute's silence deep in thought while slowly refilling his cup with another black coffee. "Professor Sully" "Please, call me Sarah" she interrupted "Sarah" he continued, "I first of all would like to congratulate you on your invention." "Well

I was really jutted continuing my father's achievements" "I wanted to ask you, don't you get scared of the idea of time travel" Sarah smiled "Scared of what?" "I mean" Ben continued with unease, "What if something goes wrong and we get trapped, or people find ways to break through the time bubble and start killing people like your great grandparents, I mean you won't exist." "Because to invent the time machine, one must understand the laws of nature. This state's time in the past has been written it cannot be changed, that's how we get our time bubble in the first place. Even if someone breaks through this bubble and kills my grandparents an alternative reality is created. I will still continue to exist and nothing of our world changes." She paused, "Ben tell me something, do you believe in destiny?" Ben pondered for a moment "I don't know, I always believe that life is what you make it. I believe life is pretty random. Why do you ask?". "Because I believed in destiny and that everyone is put on earth to do great things. I grew up believing in destiny and that my achievement and meeting you and all the people here is my destiny; and the more and more I work in the field of time and relativity, I can see this is true." "We are still given a choice, Ben. For example, just having a glimpse back in time has dramatically helped forensic scientists and thus solved a crime that has been committed. This is not for people who have been murdered and to go back and save the person's life. This is for the purpose of crime prevention and to prevent even anyone else from being murdered again. "I met my husband because I fell off my bike and broke my arm, he was the nurse that helped tendered me back to good health. I believe that is destiny. "I see" replied Ben. "Well I still think life seems pretty random anyway."

The rest of the day ended up finishing half an hour before expected. Ben made a habit of stopping at his favorite café for his usual piece of apple pie. It was a habit of habit to stop there every Friday or day that requires celebrating. Ben even had a favorite place to sit which was located by the corner window of the café which he thought was the best view in the café. He often had a usual waitress who had been serving him now for the last five years. Her name was Betty, in which during her slow period took the time out getting to know all her customers on a personal basis.

Betty came up to Ben's table and instead of asking him what he wanted to order she always asked him if he wanted the usual. "Hi Betty, how's business?." Slow day today Ben. "Sorry to hear that" "It's not Friday, so I guess congratulations are in order" Betty laughed. "You heard," "Everyone knows Ben," "Congratulations? Do you mean that or are you just saying that to be polite to one of your regular customers" said Ben "Look Ben" replied Betty "This time travelling business, I mean it's no secret that time travel is controversial. I am congratulating you because I'm proud of you and your achievements." She continued "I am worried about you Ben." "It's a dangerous thing to do for one thing." Betty stopped to pat Ben on the shoulder "And all you do is think of your career when you should be focused on finding someone to love, a girl-friend," "Time travelling does not make anyone younger, and I mean getting into something controversial. You will be famous but it won't make it easier for you to find love on this day of age." Ben smiled "Thank you, Betty, for your concerns, But I will be OK" "OK Ben I didn't mean to pry, I'm just saying as a friend" "You are a dear Betty, and yes the usual please," said Ben.

Ben woke up an hour earlier before his alarm was due to go off. He had a nightmare of being trapped alone in another time with no means of going back to his own time. Despite being aware that it was going to be a perilous day, he was excited and nervous at the same time.

It was nine o'clock when Ben arrived at Travelex with his packed belongings. He met up with all the other candidates were in the same room where he had his meeting yesterday. They started the day with a brief recap of what they had learned about the mission and then were all fitted with a vest fitted with a health monitoring device, a communications device and a tracking device.

They all stopped for morning tea before they gathered together for the mission. When they had all finished, they were all shown into a large room lighted with blue fluorescent lighting and the MAX generator located in the centre of the room. Each person in the room put on UV protection goggles. They all waited there for another ten minutes before the technician switched on the generator causing a bright light to propel out from the core of the generator onto the far wall of the room. The beam of light formed a shape of a rectangular doorway of pure light opening up a passageway in which one by one each of the crew stepped through and disappeared from the room.

Ben was the last of the crew to pass through the gateway which took him from a big empty room to a courtyard outside. It seemed a simple process to Ben, he found it hard to believe eighty years turned back in such a moment's time. Ben looked at his wrist watch and was not ticking. He turned around and noticed the porthole had closed and that was it, there was no turning back, he was locked in the year 2030.

It was a perfect day, no clouds in the sky, sun shining in the sky but not feeling the atmosphere that he was seeing. 'The time bubble must be blocking the atmosphere.' Ben thought. "Well Mr., we have a few days to look around before the big showdown," said one of the candidates to Ben. "We better get on moving then" replied Ben, "We've got a whole town to explore". They all set off their way.

The city overall was still familiar to the traveler despite the time difference. They were standing in a car parking area when they noticed people and cars all around them who did not acknowledge that they were there. Although technology had changed for them life was pretty much the same. They also noticed that the sky was perfectly blue and they could see the sun. The blue sky was a rare sight in the traveler's time. It was going to be another thirty years before the great weather shift brought wilder storms and natural disasters that led to part of the city being extended underground. The time travelers noticed people of the 2030 with generally pinker or tanned skin than they were.

"Well we've been walking around the city for a while now, so let's head to the park and break for lunch" exclaimed one of the time travelers. "Good idea, I'm hungry," said another. Ben unpacked his lunch of ham and cheese sandwiches and ate it slowly while observing his surroundings. Ben felt calm and safe at last, realising all this fear of time travelling was nothing more than hysteria. "I think time travelling will happen for everyone," said the same man as earlier before. "Excuse me" smiled Ben "Oh excuse me for my manners," said one of the travelers "My name is Sam" "I'm Ben" he replied "I'm the psychologist. They picked me to analyze the psychological effects of time travel. Do you think time travelling will happen for tourist purposes," said Ben" "Yes, it's in human nature for man to explore other worlds," Sam replied. "Well, I think it will happen as well, it seems brighter here and this world is more attractive." Sam smiled and gave Ben a reassuring pat on the shoulder.

"I think we all should separate and explore the town on our own for a while" exclaimed one of the travelers to the group. "Then make our way back to town hall when the town hall clock strikes six," they all agreed.

As a professor of history, Ben explored the town's monuments and museums. Museums in Ben's time was displayed mostly through hologram technology in which the technology in the year 2030 only was in an experimental mode in laboratories.

Ben thoroughly explored the central city museums exploring the city's historical period from 1930 to 2030. Ben scoured through every facet of the museum's artifacts and descriptions. There were no hologram displays, no virtual reality cinemas, just good old fashion displays of old artifacts in glass-sealed displays and information written with ink and paper. Ben was impressed with the outlay, "All a beautiful set up without it being spoilt with technology" Ben thought. After a while, Ben became unaware of how long he was spending in the museum. As he approached the display of the city's model, he felt a cramp in his stomach. "Darn sandwiches," Ben said out loud. Ben took out a pack of stomach ease from his pack and consumed it. He continued with a determined effort to examine the model replica of the city. He tried to touch it with his hands with no effect. His hands penetrated the glass cover and then the model itself. Ben wished he could touch something around him to pick it up and observe it. Ben was a ghost pure and simple, he could shout to the top of his lounges and nobody could hear him.

Ben heard a buzz from his receiving device from his vest. He picked it up and spoke into it. Hello Ben, this is Professor Sully. "Hi professor, checking up on me, I'm having a great time." "That's excellent news Ben, I'm glad to hear it. Look Ben we are reading that your blood pressure is a bit high" "It was the bloody sandwiches I ate, I took the packet of stomach ease already, I should feel better soon" "Ben I want you to make your way back to camp now it's getting late, be mindful of the time" "Oh sorry, I didn't realise, my wristwatch has stopped working."

Ben slowly made his way out of the museum onto the main pathway leading to the town hall. Ben had ventured out a bit and it was going to be a good hike back to the others. Ben walked on for approximately twenty minutes before he felt another pinch to his stomach. Ben leaned over and pushed his hands on his stomach to try and ease the pain. Ben made the call to rest for a while before continuing. It was a big day for Ben and the experience of all the events that were happening around him were draining. Ben stopped and sat down and reached for the water bottle. He consumed more than he should have and took another packet of stomach ease. A sore stomach mixed with stress made him realise that he should lie down for a short while before continuing. As he lay down, he closed his eyes and thought about all that had taken place throughout the day. His mind then flickered back to the day at the café and about settling down and having a family of his own. "After the promotion," Ben thought. "It must come first because I have come this far and I can't stop now". Ben opened his eyes to become once again aware of his surroundings, he noticed the sky had become darker and the birds flying in the sky were forming dark silhouettes. "I better be heading off, they are all probably wondering where I am by now."

Ben rose to his feet and stumbled, then regained his balance. He continued to walk on further. The rest proved futile, Ben felt weaker while walking back, but Ben was persistent. It wasn't long till he arrived back to the others. He was only another five minutes away from arriving at the others when he felt hit by vertigo and fell to the ground. "What's wrong with me," Ben thought. He got up to his feet again and staggered onto the streets. He stopped for a moment and heard the sound of a brake screech and turned around and noticed a car heading straight towards him. Ben quickly raised his arms to shield his head, although he assumed the car would go straight through him. As the car met up with a collision path, Ben felt the strong force of the car hit him and knocked him off his feet, onto the front of the car. Ben felt himself roll off the car and then roll back onto the road, he fell unconscious.

The sound of the alarm clock was a set of three beeps, stop, and three beeps. It wasn't loud but managed to stir Ben from his deep sleep. With his eyes closed, Ben pulled the moor down over his head to muffle the sound. 'Another day of lecturing and marking papers.' he thought. He noticed his body was aching and opened his eyes to witness an unfamiliar green cover on the more doon. Ben began to realise it wasn't his room. Ben rubbed his eyes and then sat up to have a better look around him. "Where am I?" he said out loud. 'That's right I was back in the year 2030, what happened? Ben looked at the bedside clock radio that woke him up. on 13 June 2030. Ben realised he was still back in time and everything around him was tangible. "I don't understand," he said to himself "I must have broken through the bubble". Ben managed to get himself up. He noticed a cupboard with a mirror. He looked in the mirror and saw his reflection. He noticed his face was bruised and scratched. "What happened to me," he thought. He realised that his vest and some of his clothes had been removed from him, leaving only a shirt and his pants. "I must find my vest and tell Professor Sully that I've broken through the time bubble".

Ben began to explore the room in search of his vest. It was an orderly bedroom consisting of a queen bed, cupboard, desk, and chair. It was a very sterile room, nothing fancy, with very few decorative features. Ben looked around and noticed a picture pinned to the cupboard door of a lady wearing a graduate's uniform and holding her certificate with pride. She was a pretty lady, with long brown hair, brown eyes, and golden skin. "She's pretty and smart".

Ben left the room in the futile pursuit of finding the vest in the room. He noticed a stairwell going down to what looked to be the living room. He slowly crept down the stairs, making sure he would be as quiet as he could, in order if by chance there would be someone downstairs. As Ben approached the living room, he noticed that it wasn't like the bedroom. It was a room filled with colour, decorations, paintings, a living suite, and a giant TV. "It seems as though I've been tapped in the graduate's house". Ben heard what sounded like the flickering of papers coming from the kitchen. Ben slowly moved towards it making extra careful that he would not make a sound. As Ben approached the threshold of the kitchen, he saw the same lady as what was in the picture sitting at the kitchen table reading a magazine. Ben stopped to ponder on what to do next. Ben gave out a small cough loud enough to get the lady's attention. The lady turned around and smiled with delight when she saw Ben up. "Hello Ma'am" "Oh Hello, I'm sorry I was about to go to check on you but I was off reading" "What happen?" asked Ben. "You don't remember" replied the lady "You were in an accident" "You were hit by a car" "My name is Dr. Leah Moore." "Doctor? So you brought me to your home to fix me up?" "No" replied Leah "You were taken to the John James hospital "However, we found no identification on you that could match up with our system, we could not allow you to stay there. Because you were in a stable condition, I took you home in my care instead. "So, you take all your mysterious patients home with you Doctor?" replied Ben "No just you Sir" "Please call me Ben." "Nice to meet you, Ben. Would like you like some breakfast, Ben?" "Just some coffee please" "Do you like filtered coffee Ben?" "Love some thanks" Leah got up out of her seat and made him coffee while he walked to the kitchen table to take a seat. "So Ben tell me about yourself?" "Well, I'm a professor of history. I was visiting the museum before I got hit by the car" "Professor huh!" replied Leah "I would expect the hospital would have records of a professor in our systems but you arrived out of nowhere" "I was expecting you to confess to being a ghost. "I'm not a ghost Doctor Moore" "Please call me Leah" "Thanks for taking me in Leah" "You surprised me, I expect you wouldn't trust a mysterious man" "Well my mission is to solve the mystery about you Ben" Ben blush at Leah's remark. Ben sipped the coffee Leah made for him, he wanted to bring up the subject of the vest so he could try to get back to his own time but he refrained for the time being. "So Leah tell me more about yourself" "I'm the emergency doctor at John James hospital" Leah replied "I'm ambitious and I would like to get into pediatrics. I'm single and looking for Mr. Right and I live in this old shack" "Well enough about me, what about you?" Leah replied, "Is there someone I can call, a wife, or a home you can return to?" "No" replied "I'm not married and I have no home to return to" "So I found a mysterious Professor who is homeless," said Leah sarcastically "I'm discovering more about you" "I know this looks strange" replied Ben "It's OK Ben, you can stay here until we can figure this out". "Would you like another coffee or something to eat" replied Leah "Some more coffee please" "Thanks for helping me Leah, I'm not sure why you doing this for me but you saved me and I don't think I can ever repay you" replied Ben. "You're welcome". Leah fell silent while she made another coffee. Ben noticed the clock strike ten while waiting. This reminded him to check his wrist watch and he noticed it had started ticking again. He thought about being in that time bubble and came to the assumption was because the watch stopped working. He thought about the rest of the crew and was wondering how that being missed affected the mission. Ben thought about how HQ must have been alerted by now into Ben's disappearance. He realised that the vest had a tracking device but the problem was that people can't penetrate the time bubble whenever they want and it was going to be a problem getting back home. Ben was stranded at another time and wasn't sure if he could go back home at all. All he had was the support of a nice young doctor but wasn't sure how to get on after her help. He would have to confess and tell Leah the truth and convince her that he is a time traveler.

Ben gazed into his coffee and his mind turned back to last Christmas spending time at his parent's farm. Ben grew up on a farm; he enjoyed spending time on the farm and goes back to the farm to help out his parents whenever he can. His fondest memories were of his dad teaching him how to drive the 4-wheel drive when he was sixteen. His melancholic mind was alerted by three beeps of an electronic device. "Oh damn," Leah said, "I've just been called into work". "I need to go, I probably will be back early, I want you to take some money if you go out, but take it easy; doctors orders" Leah pulled out her wallet and handed over some cash to Ben, enough for him to buy him some clothes and extra for lunch. "Thanks, I don't know how to repay you for this" Ben replied "Before you go, before the accident I had a vest" "Oh your belonging is located in the spare room located two rooms down from the bedroom you were in." "I will tell you more about myself when you get back." "I will be back before dinner time" Leah left. Ben climbed the stairs once again to head to the spare room. He needed to find the vest to get to the communication device to see if he could reach Professor Sully. Ben walked into the room and saw the vest located on a chair along with his backpack and wallet. He grabbed the vest and pressed the transmitter button on the vest. "Hello Professor Sully, Anyone" no reply, he tried again but it was futile, he could not get through. He had a GPS attached to his vest also so they could monitor his location and he hoped that there was something that they could do in bringing him home. At the moment Ben was trapped in another time, familiar and yet foreign to him. A lot has changed in eighty years. "I can start again, a new life, visit my grandparents, anyway there's a lot that must be done," Ben thought. Ben was desperate to explore the town despite his injuries. He felt fine and was in shape to have a day out. He knew he had to tell Leah the truth. "Why does she trust me, why did she even bring me here, I'm sure the hospital wouldn't desert a stranger and yet she brought me to her house" Ben was sure of the answer. Ben had a change of clothes located in his backpack and it didn't take him long to find his location to take a shower and change. It was going to be a morning of shopping and exploring the town. Ben needed to adjust to the historical setting and he felt he would have no problem with it. The main problem was the weather, he was a pale man and it was a sunny day so he would have to pack on the lotion and be mindful of the sun.

When Ben arrived at the shopping centre he was keen to find another outfit for him to wear, fashion had changed and fluoro shirts made him stand out amongst everyone else. His outfit was over the top for what he saw everyone elsewhere. People were casual and brown seems to be the norm. Ben loved shopping, he usually shopped in sub city plaza which was the liveliest and safest place to shop in the town. His current shopping ventures took place in a mall, with no virtual reality tours, no robotic shopping guides, and holo displays seen as just a big shopping mall complex. Ben felt more relaxed after spending money on a suit discovered in an all-men's clothing store. The suit consisted of long brown pants, a short beige top, and a plain brown jacket. He was so happy that he was allowed to wear it once purchased. Ben realized that he needed to eat. He wanted to go to his usual café and was looking out for something similar. He was hanging out for his lattes but the food was a must now. He was feeling weak and his stomach was starting to play up. Ben discovered a café to his liking on the second floor. It wasn't exactly what he was used to but the sandwiches they offered looked good at reasonable prices. Once he was done ordering a ham sandwich on rye and a skinny latte he managed to find a seat with a view looking out. He needed to rest because it had been a long day. He ate the sandwich which he thought was delicious and drank the hot latte which he thought was too weak. He felt his energy rising but was going to sit and enjoy the view for a while after his meal. He sat and watched the people pass by. He watched mums shopping with their children, he watched teenagers thrilled in the purchase of their new outfits and accessories they found at discount prices. He noticed people were a lot calmer and more complacent than the people in his time. One of the greatest changes that take place is the changes in global climate which dramatically affected people. Climate change made the future more uncertain and unpredictable. Parts of the city had to be placed underground for the storms that often hit the city. People are exposed to less sun making everyone paler or mustier in appearance. Life was harder in his time and he saw that people in the year 2030 were too complacent about their futures. Their indulgent lifestyles that are ruining their environment and would lead to future disasters. "I see people too complacent about their future" Ben mumbled to himself. In an attempt to avoid feeling hopeless about his current situation, he deviated his mind to Leah. "Leah my rescuer" Ben pondered. It was time to make some attempt to show her his gratitude. "Flowers have always been shown to be the best gift in an enchanting situation," he thought to himself.

He noticed a small flower shop on the third floor and took little time making his way there. He was overwhelmed by the choices of flowers that were displayed despite it being only a small flower shop. Flowers and meanings have been the subject of conversation for as long as humankind has taken the time to behold the beauty enfolded in each petal. The historical value of flowers made Ben a romantic intellect for flowers with his love of nature and taking his time to understand the nature around him. Browsing through the flower store he understood that each flower has a meaning for different cultures throughout the history of mankind. He pondered over tulips which symbolised aspiration, sunflowers which symbolised ambition, pansies which symbolised remembrance, and roses which symbolised love. He pondered for a moment longer in his choice and went for the roses.

Leaving the flower shop Ben felt tired and his need to rest encouraged him to start making his way back to Leah's house. It was a twenty-minute walk or seven minutes by bus, so he chose to walk back.

Walking back meant having to cut through the city park. The park was full of people spending the day out enjoying the sun. People were walking their dogs, picnicking in the park, and listening to a busker playing his guitar in a melancholic beat. He had to be mindful of the blazing sun and not spend too long out without risking a burn. On his way through he heard the sound of a siren leading out of the road. Curiosity got to him and decided to follow the siren. On the pathway leading out of the park, he noticed an ambulance pull up. He saw that a man had fallen off his bike and cut his leg. Ben stopped to watch the paramedic tender the injured man. This event made him feel a little faint. His mission of being sent back in time was hitting him and he felt a weight of responsibility to his journey.

Ben felt at ease arriving back at Leah's. It was four o'clock and he decided to surprise her by cooking her dinner. To his joy, he found a roast beef in the fridge along with potato, beans, and corn. He put the roses in a vase with water and placed the vase on the dining table.

It wasn't until six thirty that Leah arrived home. Ben welcomed her as she walked in the door. "Is that my roast beef I smell" replied Leah "I cooked dinner for the both of us, I hope you don't mind" "Mind, I'm so hungry and it's been a crazy day" "I'm just going upstairs and put something more comfortable on" Ben dished out the dinner and placed both dishes on the table. He sat at the side of the table which gave a view to the stairwell so he can watch Leah returns. He saw Leah come down wearing a purple evening gown. "Something more comfortable huh?" he said with a grimacing smile. "This is fantastic Ben and roses are my favorite flowers, thank you?" "You're welcome, take a seat and I will dish you up for dinner" Leah sat down at the dining table while Ben dished out the dinner. "You should be relaxing Ben, not going out of the way for me" "It's not a problem, I feel good and I want to". They ate the meal quietly together exhausted from their day out. "Your quiet Ben, I thought you would be excited about telling me about your day out" "Oh it was great, I walked to the shops and bought this suit I'm wearing" "I'm sorry I have a lot on my mind, I mean, you know nothing about me and you take me in after an accident" "I know Ben, I don't want you to make you feel overwhelmed after a car accident but waking up in a stranger's house must be perplexing for you" "A little" replied Ben. "Tell me a bit about your childhood?" "Well, I grew up on a farm. It was a hard life for my old man making a living on the farm was difficult but we managed. It was a two-hour drive to the nearest city and some weekends we would drive up to the city for the day. I loved spending time in this historical museum every time we would visit I guess I grew fond of history from that point and went to go on to study history at university" what about you Leah "Well I grew up with two other sisters in a big two-story house. My dad was a doctor and my mum stayed at home to look after us. I admired my dad and his work and being a doctor was something that I always wanted to do. I loved med school, I made so many friends, but couldn't find love. Were you ever in love? Ben?" "Yes. I had a fiancé but she died several years ago." "I'm sorry to hear that."

"Can I ask you something Ben?" "Yes. what?" "Are you a spy?" Ben was startled by the question, he laughed spontaneously. "What! No! Why do you ask?" "Well you come from nowhere and there was something I found in your bag." "What is that?" Ben said nervously. I came across what looked like a cigarette holder and then I opened it and there was nothing inside. I saw a button and pushed it and I had to say I never had a shock in all my life. There was a hologram display of a house." "Ah yes. That's a picture of the farmhouse. The one I grew up in. "So who are you, Ben." Ben became a bit nervous and took a deep breath in. "I'm a time traveler. I'm from eighty years in the future" Leah burst out laughing then realized he was serious and stopped. "Sorry, Ben I wasn't expecting.." "It's the truth" Ben interrupted. "I want to believe you but how is it possible?" "It is. I can prove it. I know things that are about to happen." "Like what." "Like next week. The president will sign a peace treaty with Iran." "That could mean you are working for the government." "Okay, what time is it." Leah looked at her watch "6:30." "Okay turn on the TV in an hour. The biggest lottery winner in history will be announced." "Who?" "Her name is Lauren Baxter and she will be almost a billion dollars richer" "Okay." Leah looked nervous and her face went bright red "I wanted to tell you that I like you, Ben." "I like you too Leah." "I wanted to know if you would be my boyfriend?" Ben's face lit up with excitement. "Oh yes, I would like that" Leah moved closer to Ben and gave him a passionate kiss. "Do you want to curl up on the sofa and watch tv with some popcorn?" "Yes that would be great" Leah raced into the kitchen and made some popcorn while Ben sat on the couch taking off his shoes. "I love watching tv with popcorn." Said Leah out loud. Leah came back from the kitchen with enough popcorn for two people in one bowl. She sat next two Ben and they started to eat. They watched starstruck on TV. A favorite comedy of Leahs. "Don't forget the announcement of the lottery is soon." Leah smiled and asked Ben if he could lie with her on the couch together. They lay on the couch with Ben wrapping his arms around Leah. "Why do you like me?" said Ben. "Because you're mysterious and gentle." Pretty soon into the tv show, there was a breaking announcement. The news broadcasted that Lauran Baxter just won the lottery. This stunned Leah. "You are telling the truth!" "Yes" "But how is it possible? "Let's just be together. I'll tell you more another time. Let's lie in bed together" said Leah. They both went to the bedroom and sat on the bed holding hands. They both felt safe in each other's presence. Ben took off his shirt. Leah noticed two sides to Ben's body. A pale bruised fragile body and a muscular well shaped strong healthy man. Leah moved in to kiss a bruise between Ben's shoulder and chest. Ben held her a little tighter. Ben made for her soft lips and kissed each other. The kiss was such a longing kiss and they both felt safe in each other's presence.

Chapter

Ben woke up the next day in a cold sweat. Leah was fast asleep next to him. He got up and walked to the bathroom. He splashed some water over his face and then dried his face with a towel. Ben walked back into the bedroom and noticed Leah starting to stir. Her silky brown hair did not seem to mess up during the night. "Hey, there stranger." Said Leah. "Hi honey" replied Ben. He leaned over and gave Leah a kiss. "What are your plans for today Leah?" "Nothing today. I'm off work." "I thought we could have a picnic today. Pack a Brunch. "That sounds wonderful. I'll get up and get ready." "Me too." Both Ben and Leah showered and changed. Leah prepared sandwiches for the morning while Ben made himself a cup of coffee. "You can tell me all about the future." said Leah. "A lot has happened in eighty years." "I want to swing by the hospital first and sign some papers first."

They both left the house and entered Leah's car. Leah sat in the driver's seat, started the car, and drove off. Be watched as Leah drove. "In my time people have automatic cars." Said Ben. "Yeah they are starting to develop them now but most people drive." Soon enough they arrived at the hospital. "I'll just pop into an emergency. You can wait there too." She parked the car and they both walked to the emergency room.

Ben waited patiently for Leah. He looked around him and saw a room full of sick and injured people waiting. He started to sweat as he watched. Within moments Leah came out and looked at Ben with concern. "Are you all right." She said, "Yeah I just want to go."

Ben and Leah walked quickly out of the hospital. "There's a park next to the hospital. We can walk there and have our picnic. You look flushed, you better eat now." Said Leah "Okay but there's something I have to tell you." Ben and Leah walked to the car and Leah grabbed the picnic basket. They crossed the road and headed to a large park. Leah threw the rug on the ground and they both sat. "I want you to eat now before we talk." Said Leah. She grabbed the sandwiches and gave one to ben. He unwrapped the foil and took a bite. "Just relax. We have all day." Ben chewed quickly and swallowed. "I have to tell you now it's important." "What is it?" "It's about my mission. I travelled back in time for a purpose." "What do you mean purpose?" questioned Leah. "My duty as a time traveler was to witness a dramatic moment in history." "What's so dramatic about this time?" "For a while now there's been global concern about the environment. Natural habitat is gone, global warming" "Yes" interrupted Leah. "Well there is a group of terrorists out there called the eco bandits." "I've never heard of them." "Well, you will today. They are going to promote their cause by launching an attack." "Attack?" "They are going to blow up the ministry of agriculture." "Blow up? When?" "Today at three pm." Leah looked at Ben surprised wondering why he didn't say this before. "We'd better go and stop it," said Leah. "It's part of history for me. I'm not supposed to change the past." Leah grabbed Ben by the arm. "The future is not written yet. We have to stop this." Ben thought for a moment and realized Leah was right. "Let's go. We can be there in less than an hour."

It was midday when Leah and Ben arrived at the minister of agriculture. Part of the building was blown up and people were running everywhere. "It's too late." Cried, Leah. "I don't understand. It was supposed to be three pm." "Your record of history is wrong. It looked as though a large bomb has only just exploded." Leah parked the car and they both ran into the building. Security blocked them off. "You can't go in there," said the chief security guard. "I'm a doctor. I'm here to help." Leah flashes her badge. "Okay, only you can come. He stays out." "That's okay Leah you go," Ben said. Leah goes into the building and Ben wanders around the building to investigate. He sees a bald man with a skull tattoo on his head and recognizes the tattoo as the eco bandits. "Hey you Mr.!" Ben shouts out.

The bandit hears this and starts running. Ben runs after him. The bandit runs into a tunnel and Ben follows him in the tunnel and loses the Bandit. Ben stops in the middle of the tunnel and looks around. The bandit jumps out and holds a gun to Ben. "I don't know who you are, Mr. you're coming with me." "Don't shoot" The bandit walks ben outside the other end of the tunnel with his gun concealed. "If you run or shout I will shoot you," said the bandit to ben. The bandit walks ben to a big black tinted van and opens the back. "Get in". The bandit drove on as Ben was trapped in the back. They eventually arrived at an old shed, isolated in a forest. The bandit opened the back of the van and told ben to get out. He led Ben into the shed which had an office table and a chair in it. The bandit opened up the shed and handcuffed Ben to a chain that was bolted down to the floor. The bandit sat on the chair facing Ben. "Are you a cop?" said the bandit. "No" Ben replied, "You recognized me", "What do you want from me?" "If the cops already recognize me and my cause, I need to hold you for ransom" "What do you mean?" "I negotiate with the police that I have a cop. I will let go of you once I have a safe passage to Mexico. "If that doesn't work?" "Then I shoot you" Ben felt terrified, he knew that plan wouldn't work. "You won't get away with this." "Well, it is the only way people will listen." "To what?" "We are waging war with the powerful. If they don't stop clearing what little habitat we have left we will continue with the attacks." "Violence never solves anything" the bandit got up from the chair and paced up and down the room. "What do you suppose you have us to do? Nobody cares." "Put on a peaceful demonstration, educate people to use the media, show the world we can achieve things with peace." The bandit stopped pacing and turned towards Ben. "It's too late the wars have begun." "No your wrong, it's never too late." Cried, Ben. The bandit looked at his wristwatch. "I've got to go out. When I come back we will go make our way to the border." The bandit left the shed leaving Ben alone and afraid. He tried to break free from his handcuffs but it was no use. All Ben could do was sit there and wait. After several minutes of waiting he felt his stomach cramp up. He wrapped his arms around his stomach and realized he was free. All of a sudden he stood up and headed to the door. He tried to open it but it was locked. He looked around to see if there was any way to get the door open. He went to the desk to see if there was a spare key. He looked in the draw but there was no key. He felt under the draw and found a key taped to the bottom of the draw. He grabbed the key and placed it in the keyhole. It fitted perfectly. He opened the drawer and started to run. He ran into the woods not knowing where he was going. He was lost. He ran until he could run no more. He then took a rest and sat on a boulder. His stomach started to cramp up again and fell to the ground. Ben started to cry. Ben heard a noise coming from the distance. He crawled on his knees and hid behind the boulder. He saw a person emerge. It was Sarah Sully. "Don't be afraid you safe. You're back in the bubble now. Ben stood up and walked towards Sarah. "I want to go back to Leah." He cried. "You can't. You have to come home with me." "Why?" he asked "Because you fulfilled your destiny." "What destiny? I didn't stop the attack." "No. your destiny was to meet Leah and give her a child." "Child?" "Yes. Soon Leah will find out she is pregnant." "I have a child." "Yes. You father my dad." "What!?" "Yes ben you are my grandfather." Ben could believe this news. "What! Why didn't you tell me?" "Because you wouldn't have believed me. There isn't much time the door leading to the future will open soon and we must go." "What is my son's name?" Ben said. "Peter." All of a sudden a door leading to a bright light opened. "I will tell you all about him when we cross. Now it's time to go." Sarah held Ben's hand and they both walked through the light.